#7 Frog Freakout

Books in the
S.W.I.T.C.H. series

#7 Frog Freakout

Ali Sparkes

illustrated by
Ross Collins

MINNEAPOLIS

Text © Ali Sparkes 2011
Illustrations © Ross Collins 2011

"SWITCH: Frog Freak Out!" was originally published in English in 2011. This edition is published by an arrangement with Oxford University Press.

Copyright © 2014 by Darby Creek

Darby Creek
A division of Lerner Publishing Group, Inc.
241 First Avenue North
Minneapolis, MN 55401 U.S.A.

For reading levels and more invormation, look up this title at
www.lernerbooks.com.

Main body text set in ITC Goudy Sans Std. 14/19.
Typeface provided by Monotype Typography.

Library of Congress Cataloging-in-Publication Data
Sparkes, Ali.
    Frog freakout / by Ali Sparkes ; illustrated by Ross Collins.
      pages   cm. — (S.W.I.T.C.H. ; #7)
    Summary: Twins Danny and Josh are having a miserable time at camp when mad scientist Petty Potts arrives, armed with her new AMPHISWITCH formula, just in time to get another camper out of trouble.
      ISBN 978–1–4677–2111–0 (lib bdg. : alk. paper)
      ISBN 978–1–4677–2417–3 (eBook)
      [1. Camps—Fiction. 2. Frogs—Fiction. 3. Brothers—Fiction. 4. Twins—Fiction. 5. Science fiction.] I. Collins, Ross, illustrator. II. Title.
PZ7.S73712Fro 2014
[Fic]—dc23   2013019710

Manufactured in the United States of America
1 – SB – 12/31/13

With grateful thanks to John Buckley, fabulous
amphibian* and reptile guru, and ARC, without
whom this book might be full of embarrassing errors.

For Maisy, Lewis and Rosie

(*And no, I don't mean John Buckley is a fabulous amphibian)

Danny and Josh
and Charlie

Josh and Danny might be twins, but they're NOT the same!
Josh loves newts, frogs, and toads. Danny can't stand them and
would much prefer to be rappelling than admiring amphibians.
Their new friend, Charlie, thinks frogs are AWESOME, but will
she feel the same once she's been S.W.I.T.C.H.ed into one?

Danny
- FULL NAME: Danny Phillips
- AGE: eight years
- HEIGHT: taller than Josh
- FAVORITE THING: skateboarding
- WORST THING: creepy-crawlies and cleaning
- AMBITION: to be a stuntman

Josh

- FULL NAME: Josh Phillips
- AGE: eight years
- HEIGHT: taller than Danny
- FAVORITE THING: collecting insects
- WORST THING: skateboarding
- AMBITION: to be an entomologist

Charlie

- FULL NAME: Charlie Isobel Wexford
- AGE: eight years
- HEIGHT: perfect
- FAVORITE THING: bungee jumping
- WORST THING: sitting still
- AMBITION: to eat mint choc chip ice cream in space

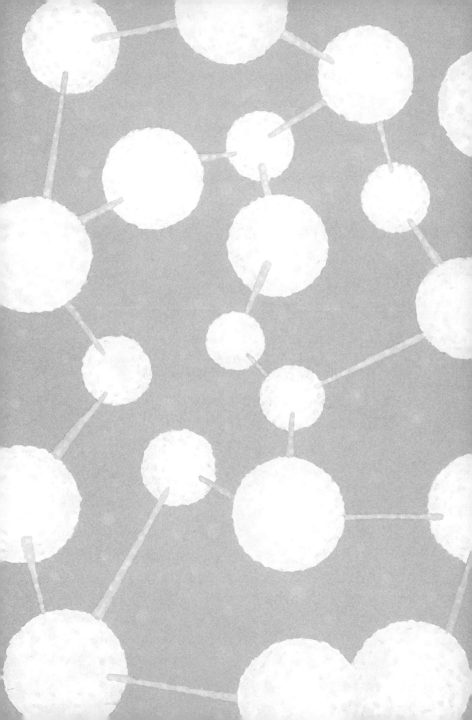

Contents

Soggy Horror

"It's raining sideways," said Danny. "In fact, I'm fairly sure it's just started raining *up*." He slammed the cabin door behind him and thumped down heavily on the bed next to Josh.

"It'll probably stop soon," sighed Josh, who was peering at a book in the dim light. The energy-saving bulbs in the cabin were orangey and not very bright.

"You said that yesterday," grumbled Danny. "And the day before."

"Well, I'm not a weather forecaster!" said Josh. "I don't know! I'm just trying to be cheerful."

"Just trying to be cheerful," mimicked Danny in a silly high voice. He kicked a bucket, which was collecting some drips from the ceiling. "Why did I ever say yes to this stupid summer camp?"

"It was the rappelling," said Josh, still reading. "And the canoeing. And the den building and the tree climbing."

Danny folded his arms and huffed. There had been *some* fun—bits of it—in between the rain. The rappelling was great. Even Josh had had a go, although he'd looked as white as a sheet in his ropes and safety helmet as he stepped off the ten-meter-high platform. The canoeing had been good too. But both these things had been cut short when the rain and wind got so bad the instructors couldn't actually *see* the kids anymore.

Since then there had been indoor stuff going on. To start with, loads of them had been playing handheld computer games for a few hours in the big canvas tepee, and that was a brilliant laugh . . . right up until Drill Sergeant had stomped in and confiscated them all.

"Didn't you read the rules?" he bellowed as the rain drummed loudly above them. "Nobody should have brought any computer games or mobile phones or gadgets with them! This is Outdoor Action Camp—not Suction Your Eyeballs

to a Beeping Screen Camp. Here—read some pamphlets on how to light a campfire instead."

His name was Steve, but every kid there called him Drill Sergeant because he was so shouty. There was a rumor that he'd been a prison guard in his last job. He had a jaw like a cement block and tiny dark eyes that glittered malevolently at kids who didn't instantly do as they were told. Several had been refused dessert and treats by Steve for misbehaving (Danny on day one!). And the man shouted so loudly whenever he was angry that the crows in a nearby clump of trees would scatter into the sky, cawing with terror.

"Ooooooh! LOOK!" Josh suddenly threw down his book and shot across the floor of the cabin to scoop something up in his hands.

"Whaaa-aat?" asked Danny, anxiously, and Callum and Sayid sat up on their bunks to see what was going on.

"What a beauty!" murmured Josh, staring into his cupped palms.

Danny stepped back a bit. He knew where this was going. "What have you got now, you freaky little bug nerd?" he asked.

"A nursery web spider!" said Josh and opened his palms gleefully. A large yellowy-brown spider sat there, its front four legs clumped together in pairs so it looked as if it might have only six. Its abdomen was long and pointed. It started to scuttle up Josh's arm.

"Eeeeeeeugh!" Danny shuddered. He hated creepy-crawlies. Even though he'd been one— quite a few times.

"Ah come on—she's gorgeous," said Josh, and Sayid came to have a look, squinting through his spectacles. So did Callum, although he kept his distance and held his Marvel comic annual across his chest.

"Gorgeous?" Danny stared at his brother. Sometimes he had difficulty believing that they really were related—but being identical twins proved they must be. "Josh . . . you need to get out more!"

Sayid and Callum soon lost interest and wandered out of the cabin, holding their raincoats over their heads, to see what was for lunch.

"I'm amazed you're still such a baby about these things," said Josh as the nursery web spider reached his shoulder. "You've *been* one!"

"Yes . . . and I've also nearly been eaten alive by one too, remember?"

Josh had to admit this was true. Over the last few weeks, he and his brother had been turned into spiders, flies, grasshoppers, ants, daddy longlegs, and even great diving beetles. And nearly every time something had tried to eat them. While Danny was a fly, he'd been captured by a female spider and wrapped up in silk—a tasty snack for later on. He was half a second away from being injected with gut-pulverizing venom when he was rescued.

"I wouldn't mind being S.W.I.T.C.H. sprayed and turned into one of these, though, for just a few minutes," said Josh. "They're amazing hunters. They don't use webs—they just hide under a leaf and POUNCE!" He shook his spidery shoulder at Danny, and Danny squeaked and jumped back. He might be super brave while dangling over the edge of a high building on a rope or turning upside down through the water in a canoe . . . but he just couldn't STAND creepy-crawlies.

"I thought you said you NEVER wanted to be S.W.I.T.C.H.ed again," said Danny. "You said you never even wanted to SEE Petty Potts over the fence. Mom thought you were really rude when you ignored Petty in the post office last week."

"Yeah, well," said Josh, gently putting the spider back down into the corner where it vanished into a crack in the floorboards. "Mom doesn't know that our sweet old neighbor is actually a mad genius scientist who's turned us into creepy-crawlies with her S.W.I.T.C.H. spray quite a few times now."

"True," agreed Danny. "She'd probably have her arrested if she did."

"Still," said Josh, "at least we're safe from Petty Potts and her sneaky experiments. We're miles away in the middle of nowhere."

"Yep." Danny grinned. "No chance of that mad granny catching up with us here! Shall we go and find out what's for lunch then?"

"OK," said Josh. They grabbed their raincoats and opened the door.

And SCREAMED.

Standing in the dripping doorway of the log cabin was Petty Potts.

Petty, Charlie—Charlie, Petty

"AAAAAARGH!" screamed Josh. And Danny
agreed.

"Pleased to see me?" Petty Potts beamed. Her
gray hair was covered with a waxed cotton beanie
hat, and her glasses were steamed up. Her shiny
red raincoat glistened eerily in the orangey light,
and she smelled worryingly of chemicals, like a
school science lab.

"What are YOU doing here?" squawked Josh.

"I was going to ask you the same thing!" said
Petty.

"We're at summer camp!" said Danny. "But
shouldn't you be doing something sinister
in your secret dungeon—like S.W.I.T.C.H.ing
some defenseless pigeons into wood lice or
something?"

"It's not a dungeon!" Petty bristled (literally—the whiskers on her chin stood up). "It's a state-of-the-art laboratory, cunningly hidden under my garden, where I perform my acts of genius. I DO wish you wouldn't be so melodramatic, Danny."

"So—why are you here?" Josh eyed her suspiciously. Even though Petty had saved their lives once or twice, neither of them trusted her as far as they could throw her (and that would not be far). Petty was just too swept up with BUGSWITCH and REPTOSWITCH experiments to give two hoots about their safety.

"I am a camp counselor!" She grinned. "I am here to look after all you small children . . . as if I were your loving auntie. Isn't that nice?"

Josh pulled Petty into the cabin and shut the door behind her. "Petty—you are NOT planning to S.W.I.T.C.H. any of the kids here, are you?" he demanded, really alarmed now.

"Of course not," said Petty. "As IF! No . . . I really wanted to get away for a while and just relax and share the company of happy young minds . . . that's all."

"So," Danny eyed her suspiciously, "nothing at all to do with your Serum Which Instigates Total Cellular Hijack?"

"Not at all," said Petty, grinning again. "I'm on holiday too. I don't plan to hijack the cells of anyone or instigate anything this week. Although you might like to know that the REPTOSWITCH formula is very nearly complete."

"How can you complete it?" asked Josh. "You never found the final crystal cube with the last bit of the secret formula!"

He and Danny exchanged uneasy glances. They had been helping Petty find the REPTOSWITCH formula all summer. It was hidden in six parts, each part in code in a crystal cube. They'd found them all—but the very last one was not in Petty's lab. Right at this moment, it was in a thick old sock at the bottom of Danny's camp gym bag. They'd decided Petty was too dangerous to have it when she nearly killed an old enemy a couple of weeks ago after S.W.I.T.C.H.ing him into a cockroach.

"Well, I'm hoping I can somehow work out the missing bit," went on Petty. "And in the meantime, as a side experiment, I've also concocted AMPHISWITCH!"

"AMPHISWITCH?" Josh couldn't help the tiniest flutter of excitement. He had always adored amphibians.

"Yes! Reptiles and amphibians are quite similar, you see . . . and although the missing part of the REPTOSWITCH formula is flummoxing me when it comes to perfecting reptile S.W.I.T.C.H.ing, the parts I have got were nine-tenths of what I needed for amphibians. I put my brilliant mind to work on some calculations, which are far too complicated for you to understand . . . and discovered the final bit for AMPHISWITCH last week! Now I can S.W.I.T.C.H. you into a frog or a toad or a newt!" Petty's eyes gleamed through the condensation on her glasses.

Danny and Josh gave her a stony look.

"But not NOW, obviously," simpered Petty. "We're all on holiday. No S.W.I.T.C.H.ing, no experiments . . . just lots of jolly FUN! So—what do you say? Shall we go and get lunch? It's pot pie and peas . . . my favorite!"

"OK," said Josh, and Danny nodded. They followed Petty out into the rain, which really did seem to be going up as well as sideways, and made for the canteen cabin.

Petty smiled happily at them as they stepped outside into a big wet gust of wind, but Josh and Danny didn't smile back. They didn't look at her at all. So they didn't see the four plastic spray bottles hidden in her coat as the gust blew it open.

Charlie was doing a handstand on a dining table when they walked into the canteen cabin. A dozen or so kids were counting and clapping. It seemed she'd been handstanding for quite some time, because they were up to sixty-six.

"Keep counting," squeaked Charlie, her face beet red and her many beaded black braids dangling between her elbows. She was wearing the Outdoor Action Camp uniform of blue shorts and a lurid orange T-shirt (the instructors and camp counselors liked to see them easily at a distance), but even upside down Danny could see that she'd "improved" her T-shirt with a Sharpie marker. The big smiley on it now had fangs, dripping blood.

"Good lord," said Petty. "Does she do this sort of thing often?"

"All the time," Danny grinned. "That's Charlie Wexford." He thought Charlie was brilliant. In the three days since they'd arrived, Charlie had been the most punished kid onsite. She'd climbed up on the girls' dormitory cabin roof and yodeled (no dessert), canoed off on her own down the river and got herself happily lost for an hour (no dessert twice and a big Drill Sergeant shouting session), cut a girl's hair with "borrowed" kitchen scissors (all her sweets confiscated and Drill Sergeant shouting for nearly half an hour)—and made up alternative words for the Outdoor Action Camp campfire song.

The proper campfire song went like this:

We love to swim; we love to climb.
We love to cook outdoors and sing.
We love to build a campfire
And be jolly about everything!

Charlie's version went this way:

We love to play computer games.
We love to watch TV and snack.
We hate this rotten weather,
And we all want to go back.

After the handheld computer games were confiscated, everyone learned Charlie's version with gusto. Drill Sergeant had ROARED at them for nearly an hour around that campfire . . . And Charlie was sent to bed without supper.

But nothing seemed to put her off.

Seventy-five, seventy-six, seventy-seven . . .

"Dear child, your head is going to pop,"
observed Petty Potts, peering at Charlie curiously.
Charlie's face was purple now.

"I feel fine," gurgled Charlie.

"Well that's perfectly all right then," said Petty,
taking a seat at the table and beaming closely
at Charlie's upended face. "As long as you don't
mind your blood pooling in your skull, leading to
congestion, vessel rupture, seizures, and possibly
death. So, everyone . . . when do we get lunch?"

Charlie looked a little worried, and her legs wobbled. Then she crashed down right into the cutlery and salt and pepper tray EXACTLY as the door flew open and Drill Sergeant strode in.

"WEXFOOOOOOORD!" bellowed Drill Sergeant, and everyone scattered away from the table in horror. Now they would ALL miss dessert.

"Hello, Steve," said Petty, getting to her feet and offering the camp leader a sickly smile. "Don't mind little Charlie here. I asked her to assist me with an experiment on the pressure of blood on the inverted brain."

"Wuff-uff-uff!" spluttered Drill Sergeant. His mouth had been open, and he'd been taking in a big lungful of air, ready to shout so loudly that everyone would be pasted against the far wall. The new camp counselor lady had taken the wind out of him . . . literally.

"You remember I told you I'm a scientist," explained Petty, taking off her hat. "So when children ask questions, I do like to explain things thoroughly to them. That's why this sweet young lady was performing a handstand. But I can see that we've been a little overenthusiastic. Don't worry about it at all, Steve. We'll soon have the knives and forks shipshape. Shut your mouth now, there's a dear." And she actually leaned over and pushed Drill Sergeant's chin up until his mouth snapped shut with a clunk of teeth. He looked absolutely astonished.

"What's your name?" asked Charlie when they were all sitting down to cottage pie and peas a few minutes later.

"Miss Potts," said Petty. "I've taken over from Miss Chatham, who, as you probably know, came out in a nasty rash of boils yesterday."

"Well, Miss Potts," grinned Charlie, waving a fork of mashed potato toward her and narrowing her dark brown eyes. "You are COOL!"

Josh and Danny, sitting on either side of the cool Miss Potts, shook their heads and groaned.

"Thank you, dear," Petty replied. "Call me Petty."

"We're watching you!" warned Danny in a low voice, leaning toward her. "Don't you try S.W.I.T.C.H.ing Charlie!"

"Danny, when will you learn to trust me?" sighed Petty with a look of great sorrow, thinking of the hidden S.W.I.T.C.H. spray bottles inside her coat. "You're all quite safe with me . . ."

Moonlit Misadventure

Charlie's most daring feat took place that night.
At around 2:30 a.m., there came a series of small
sharp knocks on their door. It sounded like a
squirrel with urgent news.

Danny blearily slid out of his top bunk, narrowly
avoiding standing on Josh's head below, and went
to the door. Outside it had stopped raining and
there in the dim light of the moon stood Charlie
in her pajamas, clutching several shiny rectangle
things.

"My DS! WHOA!" yelled Danny, scooping up
his computer gadget in delight.

"Shhhhh!" Charlie looked around edgily.
"Don't wake everyone up, you plopstick!" She
stepped inside and pushed the door shut with her
shoulder, grinning wickedly. "I couldn't sleep,

I was sooooo bored. So I thought I'd get these back for us."

Callum and Sayid were now awake. They got out of their bunks and seized their own gadgets, whooping with joy. Josh sat up in bed, smiling and shaking his head. He hadn't brought a computer game with him—creepy-crawlies were his kind of fun. "You're going to get into SUCH trouble this time, Charlie," he said. "How did you do it?"

"I noticed where Drill Sergeant left the key to the confiscation cupboard while I was in the camp office getting shouted at for the hair thing," said Charlie with a casual shrug. "It's on a hook right next to his bunk in the room next door." She held up the key, an old-fashioned iron one with a fob hanging off it—one of those soft plastic bulblike fobs with a mini yellow fish floating in red water inside it.

"I still can't believe you cut Sally's hair," guffawed Callum.

"She wanted me to! I didn't make her!" said Charlie, dropping the key back in her pajama top pocket. "Why all the fuss?"

They settled onto the bunks and switched on the gadgets with assorted jingly noises and flashes of color. The power chargers were still in their drawers so they hooked up to the mains and went on gaming for hours. Josh joined in a bit, although mostly he watched. Until he noticed something slightly worrying.

"Erm . . . guys," he said, peering out of the window. "The sun is nearly up. Don't you think we ought to get some sleep now?"

"Sheeesh!" Charlie stood up, looking worried. "I'd better get these back in the cupboard and the key back on the hook before Drill Sergeant wakes up."

"It's only 5:15," said Sayid, looking at his watch.

"But he gets up early to go running," said Charlie. "His cabin's next to ours, and I hear his alarm clock go off at six o'clock, every morning, and then he hoofs past our window ten minutes later."

"We'll come with you," offered Josh, clapping Danny's shoulder. "We can keep watch while you go in." Sayid and Callum handed back their switched-off games and scrambled back into their bunks.

It was cool and fresh as they stepped out into the dawn and made their way quietly toward the cabin that housed the office and Drill Sergeant's room at the far end of the camp. As they passed the large pond, Josh paused, entranced by a chorus of purring croaks. "Listen! It's the frogs! The froggy dawn chorus is just starting!" His eyes were shining.

"We haven't got time," hissed Danny, feeling very nervous now that the sun was so far up. He didn't fancy meeting up with Drill Sergeant while clutching all these gadgets.

"No—I want to see!" whispered Charlie and ran after Josh who was now kneeling at the edge of the pond, pointing to the little greeny-brown noses and pop-up eyes of six or seven frogs in the dark water.

Charlie dropped the games on the bank and leaned in to look. "Ooooh—they're so sweet, aren't they? Ooh—look—did you see that one go? He just hopped right out from under that rock and into the water!"

"More 'leaped' than hopped, really," said Josh. "Toads hop. Frogs leap. Actually, toads aren't even that good at hopping . . . they mostly crawl about. They're not half as energetic as frogs. They're easy to catch."

"Oh, here we go," muttered Danny. "Nerd attack. Come ON, you two!"

"Wait! I want to see another frog leap!" said Charlie, crouching next to Josh. She anchored her hands on the bank and leaned right out across the water, fascinated. There was a plop. But it wasn't a frog. It was the key to the confiscation cupboard.

Josh and Charlie squeaked in horror and tried to grab it as it sank through the water, but it was gone in a second, lost in the dark depths.

"Noooo!" gasped Charlie and shoved her arm in after it, scrabbling around frantically. Josh joined her, but all they succeeded in doing was stirring up all the silt and weeds, making it impossible to see a thing. They couldn't feel anything keylike—just the rather slippery gooeyness of waterweed, algae, and the odd squirm of something living.

Eventually, as Danny looked on in horror, they slumped down on the bank and stared at each other, aghast. "We're done for," said Josh. "We can't get the games back in the cupboard or the key back on the hook. And Drill Sergeant could wake up at any minute!"

Charlie sighed and shook her head. "No . . . you're not done for. It was me who did it . . . me who lost the key . . . you two go back to bed, and I'll own up."

"But you'll be sent home!" said Danny. "That's what they said after the hair thing. One more strike and you're out!"

"Ah well," shrugged Charlie. "It's been fun. But unless one of us turns into a frog and goes diving for the key, that's that. I'll be OK. Mom was hoping I'd last the full ten days . . . " She bit her lip. ". . . but I'm always disappointing her, so it won't be a surprise. Why are you two looking all funny?"

Josh was staring at Danny and Danny was staring right back and now he started shaking his head. "You've got to be kidding!" he said. "You have GOT to be kidding!"

Josh looked at his watch. "We've got half an hour if we're lucky," he said.

"What are you two on about?" said Charlie, peeling some pondweed off her arm.

"Erm . . . we might be able to help," said Josh, detaching a water snail from his wrist.

"Josh! NO!" hissed Danny. "You can't!"

"Look—she's not just any girl," said Josh. "She'll handle it!"

"Handle what?" said Charlie, looking very puzzled.

"Charlie—you said one of us needed to turn into a frog," said Josh. "Well . . . one of us can."

"OK," said Charlie. "If you say so."

"I'm going to tell her," Josh said to Danny, who slapped his hand across his eyes and groaned. "Listen, Charlie—don't interrupt, there's no time. We CAN turn into frogs—and we're going to do it just as soon as we've woken Petty Potts up."

Hop Till You Plop

"Which one of you is S.W.I.T.C.H.ing?" Petty eyed all three of them eagerly as they stood beside the pond. She was also wearing pajamas (thick plaid ones) with rain boots and her dark red raincoat, which she now opened up, revealing the four S.W.I.T.C.H. spray bottles held in its lining. "Frog, toad, or newt?" she added, like a mad waiter presenting a menu.

"Frog! Frog!" Charlie jumped up and down in immense excitement, clapping her hands. "Oh, I can't believe this! It's so amazing!"

"Wait—you're not going!" said Josh. "I am! It's far too dangerous for a g— for a beginner."

Charlie narrowed her eyes at him. "You meant 'for a girl'! That's what you were going to say, wasn't it?"

"No—yes—look, it doesn't matter!" spluttered Josh. "It was my plan, and believe me, you have no idea how terrifying it is to be S.W.I.T.C.H.ed. Everything wants to eat you!"

"You've done it loads of times!" pointed out Charlie. "So it can't be that bad."

"Yes, but only because Petty tricked us into it! Mostly, anyway . . ."

"Excuse me! The genius scientist is actually PRESENT, you know!" interrupted Petty. "And pardon me, but didn't you ASK for my help this time?"

"Sorry, Petty . . . but you know what I mean," said Josh.

"Yes . . . you're never all that worried about how chewed we might get, are you?" added Danny, giving her a glare.

"Nonsense. I am always filled with great concern for you," scoffed Petty. "Now—who's first?"

"Me! Me!" Charlie started jumping again, as if she was practicing. "Frog! I want to be a frog. Spray me!"

"Charlie—I said—" began Josh.

"Don't care!" said Charlie. "S.W.I.T.C.H. me, Petty, or I'll tell everyone your secret. Turn me into a frog, and I will NEVER breathe a word."

Petty was taking no chances. She pulled out a bottle with "A1" written on it in marker and sprayed it at Charlie's head. There was just time for a thrilled squeak before Charlie vanished and a frog sat at their feet, grinning in a very delighted way.

"Petty! S.W.I.T.C.H. me NOW!" commanded Josh. "You shouldn't have let her go first! If she gets eaten, I will NEVER forgive you!"

Three seconds later, there were two frogs on the bank. Petty waved the bottle at Danny and wiggled her eyebrows. He sighed. "Ah, go on then . . ."

And then there were three.

Pond Life

"Ribbet! Ribbet! Ribbet!" yelled Charlie, leaping up and down like a bug-eyed ballerina. "WOW! Ribbet! Ribbet!"

"Why do you keep going 'ribbet'?" said Josh, extending his impressive back legs and peering down the length of them.

"I'm speaking frog!" Charlie giggled.

"Right—if you say so," said Josh. "But actually, common frogs don't say 'ribbet.' We're speaking froggish right now, but the only frog which actually goes 'ribbet' is the kind in Disney movies."

PLOP! Charlie landed with a squelch, right in front of Josh. "Well I like ribbetting! Will other frogs understand us?" she asked, her bulbous eyes shining with delight. They were yellowy gold around the outer edges with large oval black pupils in the center.

"Yes, probably," chuckled Josh. He was pretty thrilled to be a frog too. "They might freak out when they see us, though. We might still smell a bit human. They might scream. They don't ribbet, but they can scream."

Danny was ready to scream at any moment. "What's going to eat me this time, Josh?" he asked, looking around edgily. Behind him the titanic shape of Petty Potts was standing very still. Her foot, in its rubber boot, looked like the size of a car.

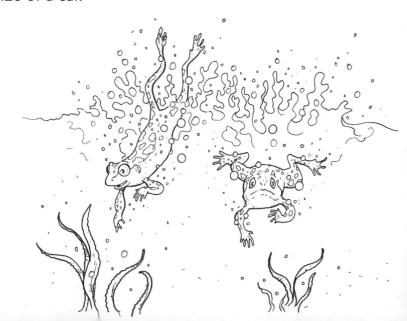

"Ummm . . . big birds might try," said Josh. "Mammals too. Snakes. A fox would make a quick snack of you, no problem. A cat too, maybe, although mostly they just like to play."

Danny shuddered, the ripples of horror visible across his mottled throat. So did Josh. He'd been "played with" by a cat before, on the day they were S.W.I.T.C.H.ed into grasshoppers. "Let's go!" he said and leapt into the water.

Two more sploshes and plumes of bubbles followed him in, and at once, the world was utterly different. They were floating through a dim watery universe, filled with elegantly wafting weed, spinning particles of silt, tumbling black water snails, and darting brown fish.

"Wooooooooooow!" marveled Charlie. "Look at meeeeee!" Keeping her arms close to her body, she kicked her long legs and webbed feet and shot through the water at high speed. Josh copied her and caught up in two seconds. "How come I can talk underwater?" asked Charlie. "I'm not opening my mouth!"

"You're sending vibrations," explained Josh, using his own vibrations. "Through your throat muscles and skin. Clever, isn't it?"

"Wait for me!" called Danny and followed close behind. "Josh! Wait! Is there anything down here which will eat me?"

Josh turned in the water and watched his brother approaching. Danny looked truly elegant. Josh had always loved frogs. Lots of people thought they were slimy and revolting, but Josh saw only their sleek, shiny beauty as they swam and their amazing leaping ability on dry land. He admired their clever pulsating throats pushing air deep down into their bodies and their amazing skin, able to adapt to water or dry land.

"We're OK down here!" he called. "There's nothing big enough to go for us in the pond. Another frog might jump on your back in springtime but not in summer. I can't see any around now, anyway. Ooooh this is SOOOO amazing!"

Danny started to relax and enjoy the cool silky feel of the water. He stopped shuddering every time waterweed stroked his skin. He noticed beautiful pale greeny-gold shafts of light filtering down from the dawn sun above, and he swam up to break the skin of the water with his nose. His nostrils sprang open in the morning air, and the scent of the pond rushed into them. It was rich and almost spicy, like earth and grass and mint. He bobbed back down under the water to find Josh drifting happily nearby. "How come I don't have to go up more often to breathe, Josh?" he asked.

"Frogs are amazing," said Josh. "We can breathe through our nostrils like this . . ." He kicked his powerful legs twice, and his nose popped through the skin of the water and up into the morning air. Danny copied him, pulling in another fresh breath

through his small nostrils. Josh dropped down
again and he followed.

"Or . . ." went on Josh, ". . . we can breathe
through our skin. That's what we're doing now,
while our nostrils are shut. Our skin absorbs
oxygen from the water. It's brilliant, isn't it?'

"Two ways to breathe!" said Danny.

"Three if you include the gills at
the tadpole stage," said Josh.

"Look at meeeeeeeeeeeeeee!" Charlie shot past
them again in a stream of bubbles and some small
whirling snails. "This is better than World of
Adventures!!!"

"OK, OK! Slow down, Charlie!" Josh grabbed
one of her legs, and she spun around in the water.

"What?" she demanded.

"Have you forgotten why we're down here?"
said Danny. "We've got to get the key!"

"The key? Oh pooh!" grumbled Charlie. "But this is so much FUN! Why don't we get Petty to spray us with loads more of that S.W.I.T.C.H. stuff? We can just spend the rest of the camp time down here! Then we don't have to worry about Drill Sergeant at all. This would be the BEST!"

"No," said Josh. "We can't! For one thing, everyone would go mad with worry. For another thing, sooner or later we'd have to get back on land and get some food. And then we might end up *being* food."

"Come on," said Danny. "Start looking for the key! We've only got minutes left before Drill Sergeant gets up and sees it's gone."

"Look for the key fob," said Josh. "The bit hanging off the key. The red ink in it should be easy to see."

"Shame we haven't got insect vision," said Danny as they swam down to the murkier depths of the pond. "When you're a bluebottle, you can look all round at once. You can check out your proboscis and your bum at the same time."

"Have you really been a fly?" marveled Charlie.

"Yep. And done fly stuff," said Danny. "And trust me—you don't want the details! You'd never eat a doughnut again."

"No insects to worry about down here, though!" said Charlie, digging cheerfully through the silt, pondweed roots, and clumps of algae. "Eeeeeugh! Wrong . . ."

Several creatures shot out of the muck cloud she'd stirred up. Danny yelped. There were eight-legged, six-legged, even clawed things, rushing towards his face.

Josh chortled. "They're just water mites and water fleas and freshwater shrimps. You can eat them if you like."

It was a menu of horror for Danny. He shut his eyes (as far as he could—they didn't seem to have proper eyelids; just filmy things) until the minibeasts had swum past him.

"What's the time now, do you think?" Josh murmured. He was getting anxious. They'd spent far too much time having froggy fun. Danny checked his wrist automatically, before realizing his watch wasn't there—just a slender, freckled, greeny-brown hand.

"I've got it! I've got it!" cried Charlie. Woohoo!" She had scooped up the key and the fob and was wearing the ring that connected them on one arm, like a bangle. "Let's hop up onto the bank then, so Petty can change us back."

They swam for the surface, but Charlie paused mid kick. "Hang on though . . ." she said, her froggy face creasing with concern. "What happens when we switch back? Are we all going to be naked? Because that is something I DON'T want to see before breakfast!"

"No, we'll be fine," said Josh. "All our clothes get S.W.I.T.C.H.ed too. Petty says the cellular hijack just takes them with us. We've never come back naked yet, have we, Danny?"

"Nope," said Danny. "Squashed, upside down, burnt eyebrows . . . but not naked."

"Good-oh!" chirruped Charlie. "Because I'm definitely S.W.I.T.C.H.ing again! It's the best fun EVER."

"Look . . . it's not all fun," warned Josh. "Sometimes it can be really dangerous."

"Oh, you're just SAYING that because you want to stop me because I'm a girl!" scoffed Charlie.

And that's when the sword shot down through the water.

Seeing Red

A second later, there was proof that frogs can scream. Charlie made the most terrifying screech as she was snagged down through the water at lightning speed. Before Josh and Danny could do more than blink, she was gone, plunged away into the dark depths. The shaft of the sword plummeted with her, and then, to Josh and Danny's horror, a plume of red came bubbling up toward them.

Josh tried to shut his eyes. He realized, with a wave of sickness, what they were seeing. He had watched a heron hunting once before, on an early morning outing with his Wild Things club. The heron had stood motionless for nearly half an hour before it suddenly turned into a vicious killing machine, driving its skewerlike beak into the water in a blur of speed and pulling it out with a writhing,

bleeding fish speared on it. A living kebab.

Charlie, he realized, with a cold thud in his heart, had just become a heron's breakfast.

Even as these thoughts fled through his brain, the huge sword was moving fast back up through the water. Something was indeed skewered on its beak. Something bleeding red through the water. Something not moving. The beak and the bleeding body vanished, leaving only a few wisps of crimson, wafting and dissolving eerily through the water.

Josh felt Danny put his webbed hand on his shoulder. "Tell me this isn't happening, Josh," he whimpered. How would they ever explain how

Charlie had died? Nobody would believe it. And Petty would never get involved at all. She would deny everything.

Josh and Danny were so shocked they forgot to move—even though they could very well be next on the menu. They stared vacantly ahead, desperately trying to make sense of what had just happened.

"Wha-what was that?" said Danny, at last.

"Heron," croaked Josh. "It would have been fast. She wouldn't have known what hit her."

"I really liked her," said Danny, his head drooping in sorrow. "She was fun. The most fun girl I've ever met."

"Aaaah, that's really nice of you to say so," said Charlie. "I like you guys too."

"BAAAAAA?!" shrieked Danny. And Josh agreed.

"WAAAAAA?!" Danny added. Josh went along with that.

Charlie grinned at them. "That was scary!" she said. "You said nothing in the pond would try to eat us, Josh."

"Bu—wha—cah . . . ?" Josh blinked several times and felt a huge surge of relief pump up through him. "Well . . . there isn't anything in the pond . . . but there's always something above it. I should have remembered the heron!"

"You're ALIVE!" yelled Danny, full of joy. "But what about all the blood? We saw blood going everywhere!"

"Nah," laughed Charlie. "That was the red ink from inside Drill Sergeant's key fob. Gave me a bit of a fright too. That daggery beak missed me by an inch—it went for the fob instead."

"Oh no—does that mean the key's gone?" Danny gulped and stared up through the water.

"Nope," said Charlie, shaking her right arm. The key and the key ring were still on it. "The plastic broke off the ring. That's all."

"We've got to get out of here and get Petty to change us back," said Josh. "I can't see the heron out there, but he could still be hunting. He wouldn't have liked the taste of that key fob."

"But if we hop up to the surface, won't he eat us?" Danny gulped.

"We'll go up under the lily pads," said Josh, pointing across to what looked like a flotilla of rounded dark green rafts on part of the surface of the pond. "We can pop up through them and then jump into the pond plants at the edge. With any luck, he won't see us. We can't wait down here any longer."

They swam in formation to the rafts, which were held together by a snaky network of underwater stems. Chinks of bright morning light streamed down through the gaps between them.

The moment Josh pushed his eyes up through the skin of water, he saw Petty standing up, waving her hands and going "Raaah!"

The heron flapped away above them.

Plop! Plop! Plop! Three frogs arrived at Petty's feet, one of them slightly clumsily, with a heavy metal key on its shiny wet wrist.

"Well done!" hissed Petty, kneeling down, easing the key off Charlie's wrist and spraying them all with some more yellowy stuff. The antidote! They waited expectantly, moving away from the edge of the pond. After a few seconds, nothing had happened.

"Oh pee, porridge, and poo!" muttered Petty, her gigantic face screwing up in annoyance. "I've brought the wrong bottle out! That's another bottle of froggy AMPHISWITCH. Sorry! You'll just have to wait to S.W.I.T.C.H. back when it wears off."

The frogs started gesturing at Petty in annoyance. "I know! I know!" she said, looking at her watch.

It was just five minutes to six. "Not to worry—*I'll* get the games in the cupboard and key back on the hook." She shoved the key in her pocket, gathered up the games, and was just about to dash off when Josh landed heavily on her foot and pointed up into the trees above them. The heron was there, perched elegantly on a branch, his blue-grey wings folded and gleaming softly in the morning sun . . .

just waiting for the human to depart so he could resume his froggy feast.

"Aaah. Yes. Perhaps you'd better come with me," said Petty. "Come along—hop to it."

Snacks and Snores

If anybody had been awake to see it, they would
have been amazed at the sight of a stout senior,
clutching a stack of kids' gadgety games, dashing
across a field like a sprinter, accompanied by three
frogs, leaping ahead of her in energetic bounds.

"Wheeeeeeee!" Charlie had quite got over her
near death experience and was hugely enjoying
the fun. So were Josh and Danny. Their back legs
were immensely powerful and catapulted them
about a foot and a half with each push off.

"Oooh—yum!" said Charlie, halfway through
a leap. Danny glanced across to see some long
spindly legs and a wing wriggling out of the side
of her mouth. "What was that?" she asked. "It
was like popcorn in the air! Who's throwing me
popcorn?!"

"That would be a mayfly," said Josh, narrowly avoiding Petty's Wellington boot.

"Eeeeugh!" shuddered Danny. But a second later, his tongue shot out of his mouth at incredible speed and collected another winged snack. *Crunch! Munch!* It was gone before he realized it. And it tasted good! Like Cheetos. "Aaaaargh! I can't believe I just did that!" croaked Danny, while Charlie whooped with delight.

"We're here!" said Petty, and they all plopped onto the wooden deck of the office cabin. Petty crept into the office and took the games straight to the confiscation cupboard. Josh, Danny, and Charlie landed with three small damp thuds on the desk and watched Petty carefully unlock the door and place the games inside. Up on the wall, the clock showed it was three minutes to Drill Sergeant's six o'clock alarm . . .

"Hurry UP, Petty," whispered Josh.

Petty relocked the cupboard. Then she very carefully pushed open the door into the bunk room behind the office. At once a gale of snores could be heard. Petty crept in, a huge silhouette in the dim light, and the three frogs followed, trying hard not to plop too loudly on the wooden floor.

Drill Sergeant lay on his side, snug in his pajamas under a duvet, snoring loudly. His back was turned to them as Petty reached across to hang the key on the wall hook just above the head end of his bed. On the bedside table, the digital clock read 5:58 a.m. As the amphibian crew stared at it, shivering with nerves, it flicked to 5:59 a.m.

"Hurry!" Charlie couldn't help whispering, jumping up in the air with anxiety. Unfortunately she landed with a loud slap exactly in the lull between snores. Drill Sergeant snorted, snuffled, and energetically turned over. Petty Potts hit the deck like an athlete, dropping the key with a loud thud—just as Drill Sergeant's eyes blearily opened. She crouched low down on his mat and scrunched up her face, waiting for the awful moment of discovery, while three frogs sat in a row behind her, their mouths hanging open in horror. For a few seconds, there was silence.

Then the alarm went off.

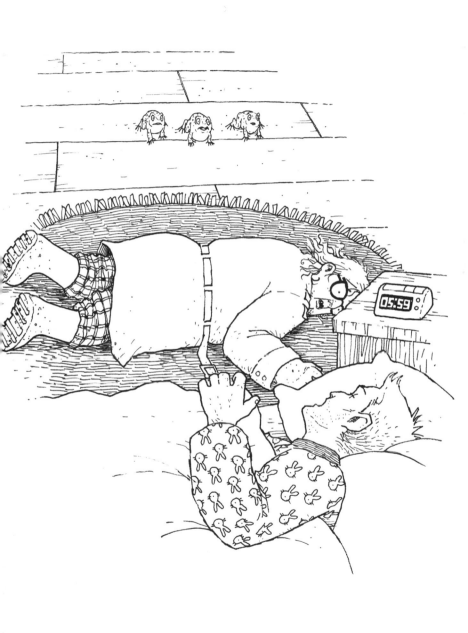

Snoozy, Oozy, Woozy

In the shadow of Petty's crouching backside, Josh
and Danny slammed their hands across their wide
mouths to stop a scream of terror shooting out.
Charlie put hers over her big eyes . . . and a high-
pitched squeak did make it out of her mouth—
but fortunately the shrill beeping of the alarm
hid it. Drill Sergeant grunted and began slapping
across to the bedside table to shut off the noise.
His slappy hand missed Petty's dismayed face by
an inch and eventually hit the clock. It fell into
silence again, and Danny, peering past Petty,
noticed that a digital word had sprung up above
the numbers, which now read 6:00 a.m. It said
"SNOOZE." Snooze? That meant another five
minutes, didn't it? Yes! Drill Sergeant rolled onto
his back and made grunty, slurpy noises as his

tongue gradually unstuck from the roof of his mouth and his jaw fell open. His eyes were shut. He was going to have a snooze!

Danny could stand it no longer. He grabbed the key from the floor, jumped up onto Petty's shoulder and then leapt for the hook. Employing all his basketball skills, he stretched his arms out and threw the key at just the right angle so that the little metal ring would drop down over the hook. Half a second later, there was a ringing metallic clink as he scored.

"Yeeeeessssssss!" Charlie and Josh couldn't help shouting. Then "Noooooooo!" as Danny landed on Drill Sergeant's face, one leg in his open mouth.

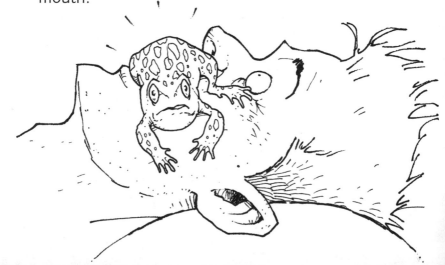

What followed was a bit crazy. Drill Sergeant bawled "Plawaaa!" and shot up in bed, scrabbling at his face and thwacking Danny down onto the duvet. Danny screamed loudly, and then, realizing that he had to keep the man's attention while Petty crawled out of the room, he did a little dance. He did a hand jive and a shimmy across the duvet while Drill Sergeant stared at him in astonishment, his mouth still wide open and his eyes bulging. He looked like a frog himself. He didn't see the old lady shuffling across his floor on her hands and knees with two leaping escorts. He was far too busy wondering how a frog had learned to disco dance.

Finally, the alarm went off again, and in the second his audience glanced away, Danny hopped off.

"We DID it!" Charlie jumped up and down outside the girls' cabin. "We got the games back in the cupboard! We got the key back on the hook! Nobody will ever know! I won't be sent home!"

"No," said Josh. "Nobody will notice anything strange at all, will they?"

"Aah," said Charlie, noticing she was still a frog. "But it will wear off soon, won't it?"

"I can't find my antidote," Petty was whispering, hoarsely, bending down from above. "You'll just have to get back into bed, all of you, and wait for it to wear off. It shouldn't be more than twenty minutes. I'll see you at breakfast!"

And she was gone.

"This has been the best adventure ever!" said Charlie. "See ya!" She jumped into the cabin through an open window, and as no girly screams followed, Josh and Danny guessed nobody had seen her get back into bed.

They got back into their own beds the same way and happily neither Callum nor Sayid noticed, being fast asleep.

It seemed like only minutes later that they were all getting up for breakfast, although it was 7:30 a.m. Josh and Danny got into their clothes and put Wellington boots on very quickly while the others weren't looking. They hurried into breakfast and sat down at Charlie's table.

"Um . . . everything . . . OK?" hissed Josh as Charlie dolloped golden syrup on her oatmeal.

"Mostly OK," said Charlie. They looked down and saw that she had Wellingtons on too, even though it was a sunny day and everyone else was in sandals or sneakers.

"You too?" said Danny, in a low voice.

"Yep . . . but it'll wear off soon . . . won't it?" Charlie eased her feet out of the wellies, and the boys glanced down to see the truth beneath the table.

Charlie's feet were still frog-colored and frog-shaped, complete with webbed toes—exactly like Danny's and Josh's.

"Yeah . . ." said Danny, reaching for the toast. "It'll wear off. The aftereffects always do—although they've never been this obvious before."

Josh grinned. "Yeah . . . don't worry. It'll be fine. No need to get all jumpy."

Top Secret!

For Petty Potts's Eyes Only!!

SPECIAL DIARY ENTRY

SUBJECT: REPTOSWITCH FORMULA

ALMOST COMPLETE

Things are going well—very, very well actually. I've been working hard on the REPTOSWITCH formula, and now it's (almost) perfect. Soon I'll be able to S.W.I.T.C.H. Danny and Josh into all kinds of scaly reptiles—lizards, chameleons, snakes, and even alligators! What a genius I am! No one else in the whole world knows how to change people into creatures—and now I can S.W.I.T.C.H. people into insects and reptiles!

Anyway, before I can share my super geniusness with the world, I need to test the formula a bit more. And I know just the two boys to help me. After all, who wouldn't want to find out what it's like to have the shell of a turtle, the forked-tongue of a snake, or the teeth of an alligator?

REMEMBER

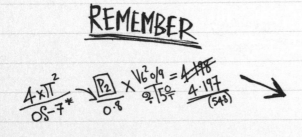

$$\frac{4 \times \pi^2}{OS - 7} \times \boxed{\frac{P_2}{0.8}} \times \frac{V_6^2 0/9}{2.15^o_+} = \frac{4.198}{4.197} \underset{(548)}{}$$

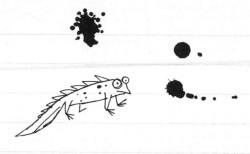

Maybe, I'll just forget to mention to Danny and Josh what happened in my earlier experiments—I wouldn't want to worry them. I mean, so what if my test subjects were not quite themselves afterward. You'd think a rat would be pleased to have constantly changing fur like a chameleon, but instead, he looked rather annoyed.

Yes, the less Josh and Danny know, the better. But I'll keep notes in my diary after every experiment. Watch out world—Genius Scientisl Petty Potts is about to take her REPTOSWITCH formula to the next level!

GET READY FOR THE NEXT SEVEN S.W.I.T.C.H. BOOKS!

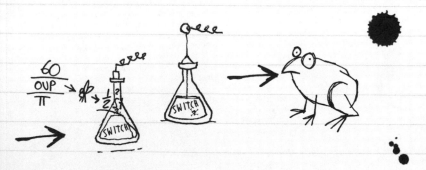

Recommended Reading

BOOKS

Want to brush up on your reptile and amphibian knowledge? Here's a list of books dedicated to slithering and hopping creatures.

Johnson, Jinny. *Animal Planet ™ Wild World: An Encyclopedia of Animals.* Minneapolis: Millbrook Press, 2013.

McCarthy, Colin. *DK Eyewitness Books: Reptile.* New York: DK Publishing, 2012.

Parker, Steve. *DK Eyewitness Books: Pond & River.* New York: DK Publishing, 2011.

WEBSITES

Find out more about nature and wildlife using the websites below.

San Diego Zoo Kids

http://kids.sandiegozoo.org/animals
Curious to learn more about some of the coolest-looking reptiles and amphibians? This website has lots of information and stunning pictures of some of Earth's most interesting creatures.

National Geographic Kids

http://kids.nationalgeographic.com/kids/
Go to this website to watch videos and read facts about your favorite reptiles and amphibians.

US Fish & Wildlife Service

http://www.nwf.org/wildlife/wildlife-library/amphibians-reptiles-and-fish.aspx
Want some tips to help you look for wildlife in your own neighborhood? Learn how to identify some slimy creatures and some scaly ones as well.

CHECK OUT ALL OF THE

Spider Stampede

Ant Attack

Fly Frenzy

Crane Fly Crash

Grasshopper Glitch

Beetle Blast

 # TITLES!

Frog Freakout

Newt Nemesis

Lizard Loopy

Chameleon Chaos

Turtle Terror

Gecko Gladiator

Anaconda Adventure

Alligator Action

About the Author

Ali Sparkes grew up in the woods of Hampshire, England. Well—not in the sense that she was raised by foxes after being abandoned as a baby— she had parents, OK? Human parents. But they used to let her run wild in the woods. But not wild as in "grunting and covered in mud and eating raw hedgehog." Anyway, during her fun days in the woods, she once took home a muddy frog in a bucket, planning to clean it up nicely and keep it as a pet. But her mom made her take it back. The frog agreed with her mom.

Ali now lives in Southampton with her husband and two teenage sons and a very small garden pond, which has never yet attracted any frog spawn or even half a newt. Ali is trying not to take this personally.

About the Illustrator

Ross Collins's more than eighty picture books and books for young readers have appeared in print around the world. He lives in Scotland and, in his spare time, enjoys leaning backward precariously in his chair.